Tulsi the Tiger
& Stories of his Jungle Friends

BEWARE
OF THE
TIGER

By Dr Chet Trivedy

Illustrated by Derek E Pearson

'For all my little nephews and nieces,' Dr Chet Trivedy

Acknowledgements

Firstly I would like to acknowledge my beloved cat Tulsi who has been by my side and will always have a special place in my heart. My dear friend Linda Hall who bought Tulsi into my life and pushed me to follow my passion around wildlife. Parita and David who encouraged me to publish these stories and whose kindness I will never forget. To Derek and George for bringing these stories to life and to all my dear family and friends who inspired and supported me during the difficult times. Finally I would like to acknowledge the men and women on the frontline of conservation who have sacrificed so much for wildlife and our wild spaces. It is their efforts that will keep Tulsi the tiger and his jungle friends safe for us to appreciate.

Illustrations

Contents

Mr Tiger's missing teeth

It was the day for Poppy and teddy to go to the zoo. They saw monkeys and elephants, giraffes and even a dancing bear. Then Poppy stood in front of a small house with a garden and a sign that read: 'Beware of the Tiger!'

An old tiger in a stripy waistcoat sat in the garden in his favourite rickety rocking chair drinking dandelion tea.

'Hello Mr Tiger, are you going to eat me?' whispered Poppy, holding teddy tightly.

'Certainly not,' croaked the old tiger. 'You see I have lost all my teeth, and besides, it's Tuesday. So, I have pickled egg and cucumber sandwiches.'

'Yuewww!' shrieked Poppy pinching teddy's nose in disgust. 'We don't care for cucumbers, or pickled eggs.' Then she asked, 'What happened to your teeth?'

The tiger explained, 'I lost them in my home in the jungle and I can't find them anywhere.'

The tiger was sad whenever he thought of the friends he had left behind in the jungle. The rhinos, tigers and lions he had grown up with had all disappeared, and he was the very last tiger. All on his own, he had to move to his small house in the zoo. He was happy there, but he missed his friends and he missed his lovely white teeth.

1

'Teddy and I will help you find your teeth, it will be an adventure,' said Poppy very excited, but a little bit scared too. So, she closed her eyes and held his paw and off they went on a magical journey to look for Mr Tiger's teeth.

When Poppy opened her eyes, they were deep in the jungle, or, at least, so she thought. It was much smaller than Mr Tiger remembered, and all that was left of the animals was an old elephant wearing a silver turban who spent his days meditating while sitting cross-legged under the last banyan tree.

Poppy whispered, 'Excuse me, sorry to bother you, but have you seen Mr Tiger's teeth?'

The elephant slowly opened his eyes and shook his head. 'All that's left of the jungle is this old tree and me, now. Maybe you should try asking in the supermarket next door? They may be able to help you.'

So, off they went to the supermarket next door to look for Mr Tiger's teeth. They found plenty of tins of soup, poppadoms, and even a mop, but no teeth. They asked the manager if he knew where they might find Mr Tiger's teeth.

The manager shook his head and said, 'Try the clothes shop next door, they may be able to help you.'

So, off they went to the clothes shop next door to look for Mr Tiger's missing teeth. The shop was full of colourful clothes. There were suits and jackets and brightly coloured saris. Mr Tiger thought he would try one on. Poppy laughed and so did teddy.

'You look silly,' she giggled. 'A tiger in sari! What a sight.'

They asked the shopkeeper if he knew where they could find Mr Tiger's teeth. He scratched his head and suddenly had an idea. 'You should go to the medicine shop next door! Surely they will be able to help you.'

So, off they skipped to the medicine shop next door. It was a curious place full of jars from floor to ceiling. A man behind the counter, who was wearing a white coat and glasses, asked if he could be of help.

'Excuse me,' said Poppy. 'We're looking for Mr Tiger's teeth, can you help?'

'Let me think,' said the man. 'We have cat's whiskers and frog's legs, but no tiger's teeth I'm afraid.'

Poppy didn't like the medicine shop, it smelt funny.

Then the man in the white coat had an idea. 'Why don't you go to see the toymaker? He's very old now, but he's been making toys for all the children in the nearby village for years. I'm sure he will be able to help you.'

They went to the toymaker's shop in the jungle where an old man with white hair and a long beard sat making a wooden horse. His shop was full of toys and even a small zoo full of wonderfully carved animals.

3

'How may I help you young lady?' he asked.

'Erm,' whispered Poppy. 'Well, you see, Mr Tiger has lost his teeth and we were wondering if you could make him some new ones?'

The old toymaker screwed up his eyes and peered closely at the tiger. Years of working in the poor light in the shop had affected his eyesight and now he could barely see at all.

He sighed. 'Once the computers came no-one wanted to buy my toys anymore. I make them now just to pass the time.'

Poppy looked at the mountains of toys stacked to the ceiling.

'But, they're beautiful,' she breathed, picking up a red wooden train she had instantly fallen in love with.

The toymaker smiled. 'I've made lots of trains and plenty of planes, but I've never made any teeth before. Come over here and let me see you, laddie.'

And with that he beckoned the tiger to come closer. He started to feel Mr Tiger's face like an artist. Mr Tiger became very ticklish while the toymaker felt his whiskers, his nose and then his mouth to make sure that his teeth would fit perfectly.

After a few minutes he had finished his measurements and then set out with his tools to make Mr Tiger his new teeth. The saw buzzed, the hammer banged, and the chisel chipped and whizzed. After what seemed forever he was ready with Mr Tiger's new teeth.

'Here you go,' he grinned. 'You can take them to the kind dentist man around the corner and he will fit them for you.'

As they were leaving, he picked up the red steam engine Poppy had been admiring, and he handed it to her. 'Here you are, young lassie. This is for you. I'm so happy you like it.' Poppy was over the moon. She loved trains, and this one would be her favourite.

Mr Tiger didn't like dentists. Nope, not one bit. He thought they were mean and wanted to hurt him, and so he was very scared. But Poppy told him that she and teddy would hold his paw, and that he would be okay.

The dentist man was very kind indeed, and he really liked animals – especially tigers – and he gave Mr Tiger a great big welcoming hug. He also looked at Poppy's teeth, congratulated her, and gave her a special sticker. Teddy wanted a sticker too, so he opened his mouth as wide as he could. The nice dentist smiled and gave teddy his sticker too.

And then it was Mr Tiger's turn to have his teeth fitted. He gave the dentist his teeth and sat down in the dental chair. Poppy held his paw and he slowly opened his mouth wide. It got wider and wider until it was so wide that the kind dentist's head completely disappeared into the tiger's mouth. In there, he clinked and clunked for almost an hour before he was finished.

'There, it's done, you can smile now,' he said.

Mr Tiger was delighted with his sparkly new teeth. He opened his mouth and let out a ferocious ROOOOOOAAR! The banyan tree shook, and Mr Elephant's turban flew off his head.

The tins of soup fell off the shelves in the supermarket. 'What a mess,' said the shopkeeper. And he shut the shop down and went back home to the city.

All the saris flew out of the clothes shop. 'What a mess' said the clothes shopkeeper. And he too shut his shop and went back home to the city.

All the jars in the medicine shop fell down and smashed on the floor. 'What a mess,' said the medicine man in the white coat. And he also shut his shop down and went back home to the city.

Mr Elephant, who had been meditating, had heard Mr Tiger's roar and he smiled a big happy elephant smile. Poppy's hair stood on end and teddy decided to hide under Poppy's coat. Mr Tiger, whose name was Tulsi, smiled and reached out his paw to hold Poppy's hand. She closed her eyes, opened them, and they were back at the zoo once more.

Tulsi was tired after their adventure. He sat back in his chair and closed his eyes; and he thought of all the wonderful friends he had grown up with in the jungle: Girish, Darshan, Hanu and Lalit, Veena and Nagin, and Tagore.

Poppy squeezed his paw gently before she went home, and she left teddy behind so Mr Tiger wouldn't be alone anymore. He smiled happily at her while he rocked in his old rocking chair, and Poppy promised she would come and visit him again very soon, so she could hear more about the adventures of Mr Tiger and his jungle friends.

Girish the Grumpy Gaur

It was Poppy's birthday and she was excited because she was going to the zoo. Mr Tiger had remembered her birthday and baked her a small cake, while teddy had got her a new train from the Internet.

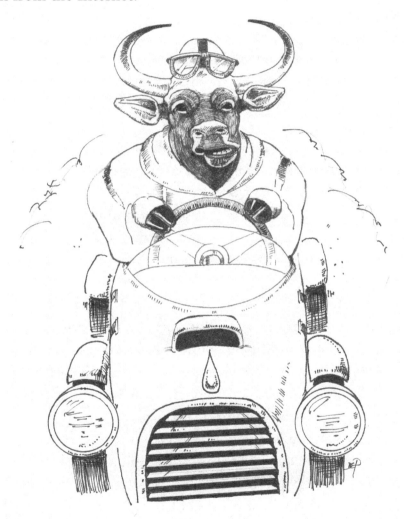

'Do animals in the jungle have birthday parties?' asked Poppy.

Mr Tiger thought about it, 'Well, some do, but others, like Girish the Gaur just don't like birthdays at all.'

7

'What no balloons or jelly?' said Poppy.

Mr Tiger replied, 'Let me tell you the story about Girish the grumpy Gaur.'

• • •

Girish was feeling particularly grumpy that morning It was too hot, the flies were annoying him, and he was in a bad mood, a very bad mood indeed.

He swished his tail and shook his big horns to shoo away the pesky flies. He didn't like flies – in fact he didn't like anyone or anything. His favourite pastime was to sit in his little waterhole all day to dream about becoming a racing car driver and visit all the wonderful places around the world.

Although Girish couldn't read he loved to look at all the pictures of sports cars in the magazines tourists often left behind when they visited. He dreamt of racing round a racetrack in a bright red, shiny sports car.

There was a reason why he was in a particularly bad mood today. Today was his birthday. He hated birthdays. He didn't like parties, balloons or even cake! Every year his friends would throw a surprise party and he would try his best to get out of going.

Last year he had put some leaves on his head and pretended he was a tree, and once he had stayed in the waterhole all day until it went dark and his friends went home crying because he hadn't even come out to blow out the candles on his cake.

The other things that made him grumpy were that he just didn't like the hot weather, or the awful litter people left behind. And worst of all was the hordes of tourists with their cameras taking pictures all day.

'Look at that cute cow,' they would point and say.

'I'm not a cow, I'm a gaur!' he would snort, grumpily.

No wonder he was in such a bad mood. He wished aloud that he could go somewhere, anywhere, that was just a bit cooler. What Girish didn't know was that he wasn't alone in his little home. On the lily-pad in the middle of the waterhole sat a little frog, and she wasn't just any old frog. She was his froggy Godmother, complete with a sparkly wand with which she could make his birthday wishes come true.

8

So, she waved her magic wand and in a puff of smoke Girish the Gaur disappeared from his waterhole to find himself in a white snowy paradise where there was no waterhole, no jungle, and, best of all, no people with annoying cameras.

The whole place was covered in white frosty powder. He hadn't seen snow before and was puzzled at how soft and cold it was. He licked a snowflake that was floating near his nose. It made him tingle all over. He tried another and then another. *Who would live in a place like this?* he wondered.

Just then a creature that looked a bit like him but had a long, shaggy white coat from head to toe appeared from out of the snow.

'Hello,' he said to the shivering Gaur. 'My name is Tanu the Takin. Welcome to the Himalayas! You must be cold, you've got no clothes on.'

'Y-yes! It's a b-bit ch-chilly isn't it,' Girish stuttered, his teeth chattering.

'Don't worry, I always carry a spare coat' said Tanu, and he gave Girish a big thick shaggy coat as well as a matching hat and scarf from his backpack. 'There you go you will fit right in now.'

Then Tanu said, 'I'm going to the yeti races. It's the event of the season, would you like to go with me? There will be a fabulous funfair, racing cars, and lots of ice-cream.'

'Racing cars?' Girish couldn't believe his ears. He had heard of the yeti races – they were famous all over the world. So off they went through the howling wind and freezing snow until they came to the entrance to a small cave which was marked with a sign at the entrance. 'What does it say?' asked Girish. 'Welcome to Yetiland – no cameras allowed,' replied Tanu. Girish was pleased to hear that.

When they entered the cave it opened up into the biggest indoor wonderland he could have ever imagined. There were merry go-rounds, a giant Ferris wheel and little yeti children running and playing on a giant bouncy castle.

Yeti families were having picnics, and best of all there was a racing track right in front of his very eyes. Girish was excited, he hadn't seen a real racing car before and he watched the drivers get ready for the grand final of the yeti races.

One of the yetis in a red jump suit approached Tanu. He looked very worried.

'Sorry to bother you,' he said, 'but one of our drivers has a backache and cannot carry on for the final race. Can you help us?'

Tanu shrugged his shoulders, 'I retired from racing years ago, but maybe my friend Girish could help?'

Girish jumped high in the air. 'Woohooooo' he snorted. This was his big chance to finally race the car of his dreams. He took off his shaggy coat, put on the red jump suit and crash helmet Mr Yeti had given him, and got ready to have the race of his life.

Ready... Steady... Race... And they were off!

The cars set off and there was a deafening noise as the engines roared, and round and round the track they went. Girish whizzed and snaked his way around the track and he left all the other cars behind. All the yetis who were watching screamed and cheered Girish as the new champion came to win the final lap. Girish was crowned the winner of the Yeti races.

The two friends posed with the yeti cup and celebrated with double helpings of chilly-chocolate and yeti-berry ice-cream. Girish thought it was the best birthday ever, and he had made so many new friends in Yetiland, but he missed his little waterhole in the jungle and he felt a bit homesick.

Just then his little froggy Godmother appeared – she had been with him all the time. She waved her magic wand and before he knew it Girish was back home in the jungle. From that day on Girish was less grumpy; and was even known to have a little dance on his birthday.

One day, in a magazine, he saw a picture of a famous racing car with two red gaurs on the side. He discovered that not only did the Gaur have a famous energy drink named after him, but he had also become the hero of a popular formula one racing team which had the two friends (Girish and Tanu) as their logo.

Darshan the Lazy Dhole

It was Poppy's Christmas holiday and she was looking forward to getting her presents. She had written a letter to Santa and asked him if Mr Tiger and teddy could come and live with them in their house in the city. Mummy didn't think it was a good idea, especially now that Poppy had a little sister.

'And where would Mr Tiger sleep?' asked daddy.

'Oh well, I will go and see him tomorrow,' Poppy said looking very sad.

The zoo was also getting ready for Christmas. There was a huge fir tree in the middle of the zoo and presents of all shapes and sizes underneath.

'Did you celebrate Christmas in the jungle, Mr Tiger?' asked Poppy.

'Oh no,' he replied. 'Christmas is for humans. We celebrate the festival of Tarabaloo,' he explained. 'And in fact, it's tonight!'

'TARABALOO? I've never heard of that,' giggled Poppy. 'What is Tarabaloo?'

She was curious to hear more as she sat on the little bench outside the tiger enclosure. Mr Tiger closed his eyes and smiled as he thought of how he and his friends had celebrated the night of the great festival. Tarabaloo was the great star bear who lived in the sky. Once every year she would come down and visit the jungle and all the creatures who lived in it.

On the night when there was no moon she would creep out of the night sky so as not to wake her baby bear, who was fast asleep, and she would put her huge bear arms around the jungle so that it became completely invisible to humans.

The animals would come out and sing and dance all night to the tunes she would play on her magic flute. The animals would play until dawn, when it would be time for Tarabaloo to go back home to her baby bear in the sky.

Mr Tiger had never met the great bear, but he knew of a little Dhole who had helped the great bear one night.

'What's a Dhole?' asked Poppy. She had never heard of a Dhole before.

'Let me tell you about Darshan, the lazy Dhole,' said Mr Tiger as he took a sip of his dandelion tea.

• • •

'Wake up it's time for school' said Mummy Dhole.

'Five more minutes, please' begged the little Dhole, 'I'm too tired to get up.'

'Brush your teeth' said Mummy Dhole.

12

'I'm too tired, I will do it tomorrow' he whined.

'Don't forget to wash behind your ears' shouted Mummy Dhole.

'I'm too tired' protested Darshan 'I'll do it tomorrow.'

'Have you done your homework?' asked Mummy Dhole.

'I'm too tired, I'll do it tomorrow.'

But tomorrow never came. Mr Owl his teacher was cross, and Darshan often had to stay behind after school to finish his homework. Darshan would also leave muddy paw prints all over the house when he came home from playing with his friends. His room was always a mess and he never combed his hair. He was a *very* lazy Dhole.

Then, one night when everyone was asleep, Darshan heard a strange sound outside his bedroom window. It sounded like someone was weeping. He tiptoed to the window and peeked outside to take a look.

To his surprise he saw a giant bear with black velvet fur that was as thick as night itself, and with big white eyes that shone like sparkling diamonds. Tears flowed like little streams from her eyes as she sat and gazed up at the sky.

Darshan, being a brave little Dhole, thought he would investigate. So, he crept quietly out of the house to see what all the fuss was about.

'Hello, I'm Darshan the Dhole,' he announced to the great bear.

The bear had a kind face, and Darshan liked her already. 'Hello,' she replied in a deep booming voice between her sobs. 'My name is Tarabaloo, but you can call me Tara. I'm meant to be going back home to my baby bear in the sky, but there is just so much smog from the city that I can't see the stars to find my way.'

She wept, 'It will be dawn soon and I if don't get home before the sun rises I will be stuck here forever and my little baby bear in the sky will be all alone.'

Darshan had always been good at finding things. He decided he would help Tarabaloo find her way home. So, he put his nose to the ground and he started to sniff his way around the jungle looking for a way to get through the smog.

It was hard work, but they had fun as they travelled around the jungle, singing and dancing. Some of the animals had left biscuits and milk for them, which Darshan enjoyed very much.

But it was a long night. He became very tired, and his poor nose was sore from all that sniffing. Then, at last, he found a little clearing in the trees and the little Dhole's tail pointed straight up at the north star which shone brightly in the sky. They danced with joy because Tarabaloo had finally found the star that would guide her home safely.

She thanked Darshan as she melted away into the night sky and took her place amongst the stars. It was way past Darshan's bedtime, and so, with a little yawn, Darshan went home. He climbed in through his bedroom window and fell fast asleep on the windowsill. It seemed barely five minutes before he heard Mummy Dhole calling him.

Darshan, wake up, it's the Tarabaloo holiday today!'

The festival of Tarabaloo was to animals what Christmas, Diwali, Hanukkah and Eid are for humans. All the animals, big and small, would meet in the jungle and exchange presents. Then at midnight they would all hold hands, say a short prayer, and light a little candle to keep their jungle safe for another year.

This was the Tarabaloo prayer:

'*Oh, Great Star Bear, we, your children, ask you, please hear our prayer.*

Protect our home as we sleep and play.

Protect our food, and the young and weak so they don't stray.

Our little jungle is all we have,

Dear Mother, please, give us your blessing on this Tarabaloo day.'

'Baloo Ho!' They would say to every creature they passed. The animals would rub noses and waggle their tails.

Darshan heard his mummy and opened his eyes. *Five more minutes, I'm too tired to get up* he thought, but then, from the corner of his sleepy little eyes, he saw a shiny diamond on his pillow. It sparkled brightly like a little star.

His face lit up with excitement. `A present for me!' he shrieked and jumped out of bed. He brushed his teeth, washed behind his ears, and rushed downstairs to show everybody his present from Tarabaloo. That night he sat on his windowsill and gazed up at the great bear and the little bear in the sky – and they looked down upon the little Dhole cub.

To this day, whenever little Dhole's play, their tails point up to the sky when they remember the night Darshan met the great star bear, Tarabaloo.

• • •

Poppy had liked the story of how Darshan had met Tarabaloo so much that she nearly forgot to give Mr Tiger his Christmas present. She put her hand in her pocket and pulled out a red silk handkerchief. She handed it to Mr Tiger who was most impressed with his present, and he placed it neatly into his waistcoat pocket.

'Baloo-Ho!' Poppy said.

'Merry Christmas to you, young Poppy,' he replied as he patted her on the head. 'I haven't bought you a present, but I thought you might like this.'

He went into his house and came back with a little book in which he had written all his stories.

'I want you to have this,' he said. 'It contains all the stories about all my jungle friends. And I will read some more to you the next time you visit.'

16

Lalit the Brave Lion

It was a bright sunny day the next time Poppy came to the zoo. She had grown taller and was wearing a tracksuit and a pair of sparkly blue trainers.

'It's not fair,' she whined. 'Why do I have to go and play rounders for the school team today? I want to stay here and listen to another story,' she said, with a big frown on her face.

Mr Tiger looked at her new trainers. 'My fiend Lalit had trainers just like yours,' he said.

'Did he play rounders too?' asked Poppy.

'Oh yes,' said Mr Tiger. 'He was good at every sport. I tell you what, there's just time for one more story before you need to go for your match.'

And he told her about Lalit, the brave Lion.

Lalit was the bravest and fastest of all the young animals in the jungle. At school he always won first prize on sports day, and his sister Leela had been the fastest runner in the jungle marathon for three years in a row.

17

Then one day Lalit didn't feel well. He had woken up in a cold sweat, his throat hurt, and his legs were really sore. He just wanted to stay in bed and peek at the day from under the covers.

'It's your sports day soon, Lalit,' said Mummy Lion.

'I'm not feeling too good,' said Lalit, licking at his paws which were swollen and sore.

'Oh dear,' said Mummy Lion. 'Then it's off to Dr Rhino's office for you today. I will make an appointment.'

So off they went to see the doctor. The kind receptionist gave Lalit a lollipop and a book to read while they waited for the busy Dr Rhino, who had a long queue of animals to see that morning.

Mr Tiger was there with a toothache, Hanu the langur had a sore tummy, and Darshan had tripped over his untied shoe-laces and bumped his head! What a silly Dhole.

Finally, it was Lalit's turn to see Dr Rhino.

'Open wide,' said Dr Rhino.

'Aaaaaaghhhhh!' Said Lalit.

'Hmmmm, I see.' said Dr Rhino and he scribbled it all down in his diary. Next, he listened to Lalit's chest with his stethoscope. 'Hmmmm' said Dr Rhino again, and he scribbled it all down in his diary once more. 'We need to do some more tests,' said Dr Rhino. 'And then we will know what to do.' With that he waved them goodbye and sent Lalit to go and have his blood test.

Lalit was scared. He didn't like doctors or needles. Nurse Nilgai, who was very nice and very gentle, said she would put on some magic cream first and give him a special certificate for being brave.

The blood test didn't hurt, not one bit and it was all done in no time.

A few days later it was time to go back to see Dr Rhino for Lalit's results. Dr Rhino looked down at the results through his half-rimmed spectacles and said, 'Hmmmm.' And he scribbled them all down in his diary.

He put his arm around the little lion. 'Lalit, you see, your blood is made of red cells which carry oxygen around your body – and white cells which fight all the germs and infections. Your blood tests show that your white cells are out of control, and we will need to give you some special medicine to make you well once more.'

So, off they went to the medicine shop to get Lalit's medicine. It tasted horrible, so Mummy Lion gave him two scoops of chocolate ice cream to make it all better. But Lalit didn't like his medicine, not one bit.

A few days later Lalit woke up and brushed his teeth. He had his bath not forgetting to wash behind his ears. But when he went to comb his hair and looked in the mirror it had all fallen out – every last hair on the top of his lovely lion's head was gone. Lalit was so upset he began to cry.

Mummy Lion gave him a big hug. 'It's okay. You are my brave little lion and you will be just fine.'

He wept, 'But it's the sports day next week! What shall I do? All the other animals will laugh at me!'

'Don't worry,' said Mummy Lion. 'We will go to the clothes shop. I'm sure they will be able to help us.'

In the shop, they found hats of all colours, shapes and sizes. The man in the shop was very helpful and didn't laugh at the hairless lion.

'Young sir,' he said politely. 'May I interest you in this top hat?' And he tried it on for size.

Lalit looked in the mirror and smiled. 'I think it's nice, but I can't jump wearing this.' And he shook his head and gave it back.

'How about this, then?' said the man and gave him a silver turban.

Lalit tried it on, and although it was a turban fit for a prince the lion shook his head. 'I can't run wearing this,' he said, and he politely gave it back.

'I know,' said the man from the shop. 'I have the perfect hat!'

And he gave Lalit a green baseball cap. Lalit tried it on, and it *was* perfect.

Soon it was time for Lalit's sports day. All the animals were there warming up for the big events. Lalit was feeling very embarrassed and he hid himself behind his mummy just in case someone saw that he had lost all of his hair.

'Don't worry,' said Mummy Lion. 'It will be just fine.'

All the animals started to compete. First came the sack race, followed by the egg and spoon race. Then it was Lalit's turn to enter the jungle marathon.

Ready... Steady... And they were off!

Lalit's legs hurt, and he was feeling very tired, and although he pushed as hard as his legs could carry him, he just had no energy. It was hard work, but he kept going. All the other animals had long completed their races when he finally crossed the finishing line.

Lalit felt sad that he had come last, and he took off his cap to wipe the sweat from his brow. All the other animals saw that he had lost his hair. The stadium went quiet. You could hear a pin drop. Lalit felt ashamed.

However, one by one, all of the other animals came and gave him a big hug. They all realised what had happened to Lalit and they all cheered him. They lifted him high on their shoulders like the true hero he was. There were cheers wherever he went. 'Hip, Hip, Hooray!' they all shouted.

So, although he didn't win his race, Lalit was still the bravest lion in the whole jungle and everyone loved him.

Hanu the Greedy Langur

Mr Tiger watched Poppy eat her third chocolate bar in a row. He looked at the young girl, frowning at her over his rimmed spectacles.

'Be careful, you'll end up like Hanu the little monkey,' he warned her.

'I want to hear all about him,' she pleaded as he settled into his rocking chair. 'Now, let me think,' he said as he thought hard about his friend Hanu the greedy Langur.

Hanu was a greedy little monkey. Even as a baby he had thought the sun was a ripe fruit and he would cry because it was always just out of his reach. His favourite pastime was to sneak out of the jungle and go into the city in search of food.

Mummy Langur used to tell him every day, 'Hanu don't eat food from the city it will make you ill.'

21

But the little Langur didn't listen, and he would have his breakfast and make his way to the city to look for treats.

First on his stop was the baker's shop.

'Hello Hanu,' said the baker. 'Would you like some fresh bread I just baked?' 'No thank-you,' said Hanu. 'I've just had breakfast, but I will try one small piece.'

And with that he finished the whole plate of delicious fresh bread.

Next, he went to the pizza take-away where they were baking fresh hot pizzas.

'Hello, Hanu, would you like some pizza?' asked the man. `

'No thank-you' said Hanu. 'I've just had some bread, but I will try a tiny slice just to see what it tastes like.'

And with that he ate the whole pizza.

Hanu passed by his favourite sweet shop there were lots of Indian sweets on display. There were jalebis, barfis and ladoos, which were his favourite treats. 'Welcome, Hanu. Would you like to try some sweets?' asked the shopkeeper.

'Oh no, I really shouldn't,' said Hanu. 'I've just had pizza, but I will try just a small piece.'

And with that he ate all the sweets in the shop.

It was time for Hanu to go back to the jungle. Mummy Langur was calling him for his tea. Hanu came home washed his hands and face, and got ready for dinner. `

'I've made your favourite spaghetti with tomato sauce,' said Mummy Langur. 'Oh, Mummy, I'm not hungry, but I will try some of the delicious spaghetti.' And with one gulp he slurped the whole bowl of spaghetti.

'Hanu!' Mummy Langur exclaimed. 'You are going to get a tummy-ache.'

Hanu brushed his teeth, put on his pyjamas and got ready to go to bed. Soon there was a rumble in his tummy. It sounded like thunder and it got louder and louder. Soon after that Hanu was howling that his poor tummy was sore. Mummy Langur rubbed his tummy and sang him a lullaby, but that did not help.

The bread, pizza, jalebi, barfis, ladoos and spaghetti were all doing somersaults in his poor little tummy and he didn't know what to do. In the morning Mummy Langur made an appointment to see Dr Rhino.

Dr Rhino shook his finger and said little Langurs should only eat food from the jungle and not the food from the shops in the city, and that is why there are always signs which says 'do not feed the animals' in all the zoos and parks. He explained that human food can make animals very sick.

From that day on Hanu stuck to eating fruits and leaves, although he still enjoys his favourite spaghetti with tomato sauce – just once in a while.

Veena's on a diet

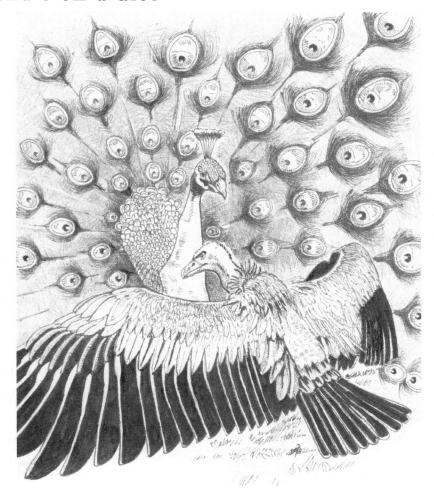

Poppy looked sad. 'What's wrong?' asked Mr Tiger.

'Everyone in my class laughs at me because of my big glasses,' she said. 'I wish I was different.'

'We are all different and all special in our own way,' he said patting her gently on the head. 'Just look at Veena, the most beautiful bird in the jungle.'

And he told Poppy the story of Veena the Vulture.

• • •

'Breakfast is ready,' shouted Mummy Vulture. 'It's rats' tails and lizard soup.' 'I'm not hungry, and I'm on a diet!' Squawked Veena.

She looked at the profile update on her Featherbook social media page. Fara flamingo, Sheela stork and Kamla crane were all posing in their swimming costumes doing selfies with a famous photographer from *Jungle Asia Magazine*.

'It's not fair,' she thought. 'I want long skinny legs, I want pink feathers. Why am I so dull and boring?'

Mummy vulture put a wing around her and gave her a hug. 'There, there, sweetie. You are a beautiful vulture. Now, eat your breakfast.'

Veena packed her lunch box with two leaves of lettuce and a small mouse and went off to school. It was the school dance next week and all the birds were getting ready for the big event. They were hoping to get to dance with Mohan, the most beautiful peacock in the jungle, who would dazzle everyone with his bright feathers and shimmering dance.

'Wow! Look at Mohan,' they would say as he strutted past the canteen. Once Kamla Crane pretended to faint outside the chemistry lab hoping that Mohan would rescue her, but Mr Owl their teacher arrived in time and gave her three big spoonful's of cod liver oil to help her feel better.

Finally, it was the day of the big dance and everybody arrived at the school in their best outfits. The Tweeter pages were buzzing with posts about who would get to dance with Mohan.

'Pick me!' shouted Fara Flamingo as the band started to play, but Mohan ignored her and carried on walking.

Sheela stork waved and called out, 'Cooey! Hello, Moeey Woeey! I'm over here.' But Mohan looked the other way and carried on walking.

This was breaking news, Mohan had snubbed the two most elegant and sought-after girls in the school.

Then, just as he reached Veena, he paused and bowed. 'Madam, would you do me the honour of this dance?'

Veena was shocked, and she blushed so much that her bald head went bright pink, and with great surprise she squeaked, 'Of course.'

Mohan opened his beautiful plumage and the whole floor erupted in cheers. They danced and waltzed the night away with the tango, fox-trot and even the quick step. Veena was a natural and all her time spent watching ballroom dancing on television had paid off.

Everyone clapped and cheered as the two danced and whirled like champions. From that day onwards Veena decided she didn't mind being a vulture and decided that she didn't need to be like the others with long skinny legs and pink feathers. She was happy being just who she was – a beautiful young vulture who loved to dance.

Nagin the Cricketing Cobra

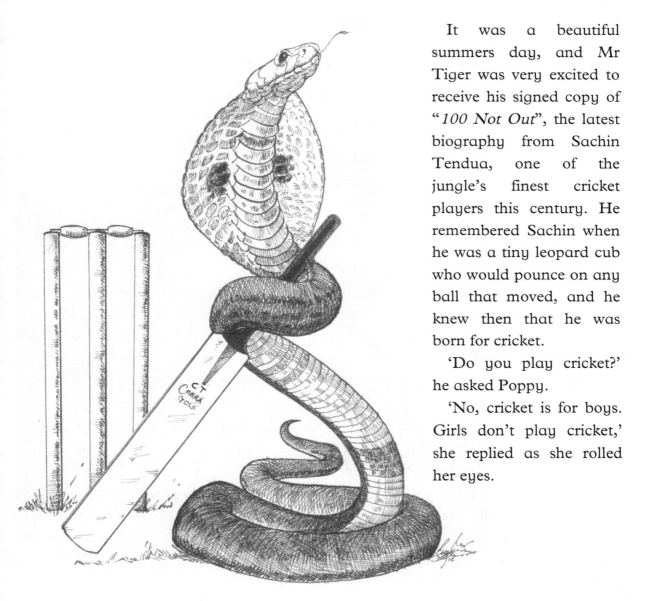

It was a beautiful summers day, and Mr Tiger was very excited to receive his signed copy of "*100 Not Out*", the latest biography from Sachin Tendua, one of the jungle's finest cricket players this century. He remembered Sachin when he was a tiny leopard cub who would pounce on any ball that moved, and he knew then that he was born for cricket.

'Do you play cricket?' he asked Poppy.

'No, cricket is for boys. Girls don't play cricket,' she replied as she rolled her eyes.

'Of course, they do,' replied the old tiger with a big smile. 'Nagin the cobra was the star of the jungle cricket team back in the day, and she and Sachin share the record for the most runs scored in a match. They put on 96 runs in one day.'

Poppy chuckled. 'Snakes can't play cricket! They have no arms or legs. How they can run?'

'Don't be too quick to judge, young lady. Nagin was no ordinary snake and no ordinary cricket player.'

And he told her the story of Nagin the Cricketing Cobra.

• • •

Nagin had curled up into a tiny ball as she peered over the boundary rope to watch the cricket match. She would take every opportunity to sneak away from home and wonder over to where the animals were playing cricket.

Nagin was the friendliest snake in the world, and she loved cricket and dreamt of playing for the jungle team. She was a big fan of Sachin Tendua the most famous leopard batsman the jungle had ever seen.

She was thrilled by all the excitement of the game and dreamt that one day she too would take the crease, but whenever she mentioned it everyone would laugh at her.

'What? A snake playing cricket? You've got no legs, how you will run? You've got no arms, how you will hold the bat or catch the ball?'

They scoffed and jeered at poor Nagin, 'Besides,' they said, 'you're a girl, and girls don't play cricket.'

Nagin sighed and slithered away to hide under a bush where she wept quietly. Why shouldn't she play cricket? Who says you need arms or legs?

'I will show them,' she said, and indeed she did.

After her chores looking after her little brothers and sisters, Nagin would go to the ground where Sachin Tendua and the other members of the team would practice. She watched carefully as they practiced in the nets. The leg glance, cover drive, pull shot she knew them all, and she had learned everything she knew from *Test Match Special* on the radio.

One day, she was watching a match when a ball came whizzing over her head. In a shot she opened her cobra's snake hood and caught the ball high in the air. The players were so surprised to see the catch they ran over to see if she was okay.

She smiled at them and used her powerful snake coils to return the ball to the stumps. They were amazed with her agility and her catching skills.

'Do you want to play?' asked the captain. 'We have a team of touring badgers coming from England and we could do with an extra player.'

'Yesssss please,' she hissed with excitement. 'But, you know, I'm a snake and have no arms or legs – and also that I'm a girl.'

'You're a cricket player and that's all that matters,' replied Mr Sambar, who was manager of the jungle cricket team. 'Besides you will be playing with Sachin Tendua and he will show you the ropes.'

She fainted at the mention of her cricketing hero.

It was the day of the big game. The badgers had arrived and were wearing big floppy hats to keep out of the sun. They watched the jungle team take to the field led by Sachin himself. Last they saw little Nagin slither behind the rest of the team and take her position behind the stumps.

Ooh, what a sight, they thought, until she raised herself off the ground and spread her big cobra hood ready for a catch or stumping.

The first batsmen started to shiver in his boots, 'There's a ssss – nnn – aaa – kkke behind me,' he stuttered, and he was out first ball and ran back to the changing room.

Nagin was in her element she threw herself at every ball, and in the end, she had made three catches. The badgers made a total of 90 runs in their innings a respectable score for their team.

Then it was time for the jungle team to bat. Things were not going well, the first four players got out without scoring a run and Sachin had scored fifteen so far. The badgers were confident when Nagin came to the crease.

They all crowded around her as she made a coil with her body and gripped the bat tightly. The first ball came and bounced nearby, she slid across and smashed the ball for four runs. The crowd went wild.

The next three went the same way. She was beginning to enjoy this. She would slide effortlessly between the wickets taking quick singles, or else smashed the ball to the boundary.

It was the last ball and the scores were tied. They needed one more run to win and Nagin was at the crease. The crowd was quiet, and some were biting their hooves with anxiety. Nagin was ready. She raised herself up on her powerful coils and looked straight at the bowler, concentrating hard.

When the ball came she smashed it for the biggest six the crowd had ever seen. The jungle team had beaten the badgers and Sachin and Nagin were the heroes of the day. From that day on she has kept wicket for the cricket team. There is also an all snake team called the Cobras which she manages, and who have been the jungle champions four years in a row.

'So, you see, young Poppy, anyone can play cricket,' said Mr Tiger with a wink. Poppy asked if she could borrow his book on cricket one day after he had read it. 'Sure, why not?' he replied as he patted her gently on the head.

Ganesh the Forgetful Elephant

It was Halloween when Poppy went to see Mr Tiger and teddy at the zoo. Mr Tiger was carving pumpkins and teddy was getting his Halloween costume ready.

Poppy looked upset. 'What's wrong?' asked Mr Tiger.

'I forgot it's Halloween and I didn't take my costume for the school party,' she replied as she sobbed.

'Don't worry,' replied Mr Tiger as he patted her head gently. 'I forget things all the time. My dear friend Ganesh the Elephant had the worst memory, and he was always forgetting things.'

And so, he told her the story of Ganesh the forgetful Elephant.

• • •

Ganesh spent his time meditating under the ancient banyan tree. He would watch the villagers going about their work, fetching water from the stream and cutting trees for firewood.

The old banyan tree, which was 1000 years old, was all that was left of the jungle where he grew up, and it was his home. Ganesh loved his little patch of forest, but the problem was that he was getting forgetful.

They say elephants never forget, but Ganesh had the most terrible memory, and he was getting old. His family had moved away, and he wasn't very good with emails, so he didn't keep in touch very much with his cousins who lived in Africa. Ganesh had lots of friends in the jungle. They would call him 'Baapu' meaning the great father. Everyone loved the wise old elephant, even though he was becoming a bit forgetful.

One day Ganesh was walking round looking worried.

'What's wrong,' asked Girish the Gaur.

'It's my glasses, I can't find them anywhere,' he replied.

Girish laughed, 'They are on your head, Baapu!'

'Oh,' he replied as he used his trunk to find his old spectacles. 'I am a silly elephant.'

Another time he was sitting meditating in Mrs Langur's tree house.

'What are you doing here?' she asked. 'This tree is too small for an elephant. Your banyan tree is over there.'

'Silly me,' he replied, 'I forgot!' And Mrs Langur made Hanu walk the elderly elephant back to his tree.

The following day he was cross because he had lost his shoes.

'They are on your feet, Baapu,' smiled Lalit the Lion.

'Oh yes, sorry,' he said, looking very sad. His memory was getting worse. Sometimes Ganesh would sit all day in his pyjamas because he had forgotten it was daytime, which made his friends very sad.

All the animals were getting worried about the old elephant and they called a meeting in the jungle to see what they could do. Girish had heard of a retirement place for old elephants. But all the other animals shook their heads because no-one wanted him to leave their little jungle.

Tulsi the Tiger had an idea. 'What we will do is this. We will create lots of brightly coloured signs and place them around the jungle to remind Ganesh of where his things are.'

And Veena the Vulture said she would use some string so that he could hang his spectacles around his neck. Soon the jungle was full of little brightly coloured signs that Darshan the Dhole had made in his best handwriting to help the old elephant with his memory.

Ganesh knew what his friends were up to and so every morning he would go around the jungle and pick up the signs with his trunk and gently leave a little flower in its place to say thank you.

He would take the signs home and put them up on his wall and every morning he would read them and remind himself of where everything was. Soon the jungle was full of little flowers which his friends would take home with them to remind them that their friend the wise old elephant was okay.

And now Mr Tiger was also getting old and he too was worried about his memory, and a fat tear rolled down his cheek when he thought of his dear old friend Ganesh.

How Mr Tiger Lost His Teeth

Poppy had grown up to become a famous conservationist. She had travelled the world and helped many rare and special animals. Today it was her turn to bring her little twin daughters to meet Mr Tiger.

He was happy to see them all and he walked slowly with his walking stick to meet the little girls.

'Hello, little ones,' he croaked in his soft voice.

'What's your name?' asked Rita.

'My name is Tulsi,' he replied.

'How did you lose your teeth?' asked Sita.

'Don't be so rude, children,' said Poppy.

'That's okay,' said Mr Tiger. 'That's one story I never got around to telling you. I'm afraid that nowadays my memory isn't what it used to be.'

He called for the twins to come and sit by his side as he gently rocked in his favourite rickety rocking chair. And he told the story of how he had lost his teeth.

Tulsi was the nosiest tiger cub in the jungle. He wanted to know about everything and everyone. He would wake up early every morning while his brothers and sisters slept in; and he would wander around the jungle looking for adventure.

He would spend hours looking at the birds and insects as they scurried around in the leaves. He loved smelling the flowers, and would be amazed by the fishes as they swam in the nearby lake.

The jungle is just perfect, he thought. *Who could ask for a nicer home?*

One day, when Tulsi was busy stalking a dung beetle, he heard a strange sound. It wasn't something he had heard before. *What a racket,* he thought, and he went to explore. He crept slowly and quietly through the long grass and peered out, just so he could just see.

There were three little huts, outside which children were playing. They were running and jumping, and some were even kicking a ball around. It looked like so much fun that his tail started to twitch, and his eyes became the size of saucers.

He wanted to jump and join in; he wanted to kick a ball; but his mum had warned him about humans and how dangerous they were. She had told him how they liked to chase and eat tigers just for fun.

But, he thought, these humans were tiny. Surely, they wouldn't want to harm his poor stripy tail? And so, he crept home quietly and kept his trip to the village school his little secret.

Tulsi would go to visit the school every day. He would listen to the teacher teach biology, maths and history. He was fascinated by it all. One day, as Tulsi was lying in the grass dreaming about algebra, a young boy came and sat next to him. The little boy wasn't scared and smiled nicely at him.

Tulsi gave him a little grin, because he thought that if he smiled too widely it might scare the poor child.

'Hello, my name is Tulsidas, but you can call me Tulsi,' said the little tiger.

'I'm Tagore,' the little boy replied politely. 'Would you like a sandwich? They are pickled egg and cucumber,' he explained.

Tulsi had only ever tried sambar, wild boar and the occasional goat. He had never tried a sandwich before. He gave it a sniff and then a poke to make sure it was dead, and then he gulped it down in one go. His tongue started to tingle, and his nose twitched, but he liked it so much that he had three more.

From then on, Tulsi and Tagore became the best of friends, and they would meet after school to share stories about history, math's and Tulsi's favourite subject, biology.

Soon Tulsi became an expert at reading and writing and even spelling. He just couldn't get enough of reading and he could read a book in a single day. He and Tagore would sit under the old mango tree and read until it was dark, and then Tulsi would carry Tagore on his back and drop him off safely at his home.

Tulsi's parents were very worried that their little cub was spending far too much time at school. He hadn't learnt to hunt, and he had even become a vegetarian. All the other animals in the forest would point and laugh at him. Who would have thought? A vegetarian tiger? But Tulsi didn't care, he was happy eating sweets, chocolates and his new favourite – pickled eggs and cucumber sandwiches.

Being a tiger, he had never learned to brush his teeth and one day he had a horrible toothache.

'Owwwwew,' he screamed.

'I told you so,' said Papa Tiger. 'That's what happens when you eat human food and don't brush your teeth.'

They went to see Mr Bhaloo the dentist who shook his finger at the little tiger.

'Tulsi,' he said. 'I'm afraid all your teeth have rotted from all the sugar you've been eating, and they will all have to be taken out.'

Tulsi cried, but how was he to know that too many sweets and chocolates were bad for a tiger's teeth? The toothless cub grew up to be a handsome young tiger with a beautiful shiny coat and a bushy stripy tail. The school made him the head of biology and even gave him a special waistcoat and pocket watch to match his lovely stripy skin.

He loved the children and he would take them on field trips where they would camp under the stars, and he would teach them how to respect and enjoy nature.

Life was great until one day he got a letter. It was from his old friend Tagore who had grown up to become a doctor.

In the letter Tagore told him he was moving to England to get married. Poor Tulsi was heartbroken to learn that his best friend was moving away. Tulsi had also dreamed of travelling on an aeroplane to faraway places, but the jungle was his home and he loved it so much.

Then, as time went by, the jungle got smaller. The villages had become bigger and the animals had slowly drifted off to faraway places where they could live quietly without the noise of the big trucks that roared through the jungle bashing anything or anyone that got in their way.

One day Tulsi went back to his childhood school only to see a bulldozer breaking down the school huts where he had grown up. Father David, the old headmaster who had always been so kind to Tulsi, stood next to him and held his paw.

He explained, 'Sorry, my son. They said we had to close the school and move to a new place in the city. They want to build a new highway with more lanes for all the extra cars and buses.'

Tulsi shook his head as he remembered the good days when he would take the children on adventures around the jungle – and now all there was, was the noise of trucks, dust and the smell of smoke.

Soon, all of the other animals were gone, and every day Tulsi would sit all alone where the old school buildings used to be; waiting for his friend Tagore to return.

Many years went by. Tulsi's whiskers began to turn grey and he walked with a bamboo walking stick. One day, as he sat writing his memoirs, a little boy came up to him and coughed gently.

'Excuse me, are you, Mr Tiger?'

Tulsi peered over his spectacles. 'Tagore is it really you?' he asked in shock. 'No, he's my daddy,' said the boy, pointing to a man walking up to them carrying a large box of sandwiches.

Tagore hadn't forgotten his old friend, and he had come to take him back to England, where he could live out his days peacefully as the last tiger in world.

• • •

Poppy and her children sat with Tulsi while he dozed off in his chair. They watched as he gently rocked, dreaming of all the wonderful adventures he had enjoyed with his friends in the jungle.

The End

Author's Note

I had never imagined I would ever write a children's story, let alone one about the very last tiger in the world's quest to reclaim his lost teeth. Ever since the age of four I had dreamt of becoming a 'zoo keeper' and working with animals. Despite a career in the medical field I have been fortunate enough to travel to wildlife sanctuaries across India in search for the elusive Mr Tiger, and after ten years of scouring jungles I have only managed a few brief sightings. These stories came to me as a stream of consciousness while I was recovering from a minor stroke back in February 2015.

With my speech and vision affected I sought refuge in regular visits to my local zoo in Dudley, and the world-famous London zoo where I would go and sit with the tigers and daydream about these wonderful creatures. It was here that these stories took shape as an escape from the realities of my life as a patient recovering from illness.

Although the aim was never to publish these short stories I thought they would at least be a distraction from my illness and raise awareness of some of the lesser-known icons of Indian wildlife such as the Gaur, Dhole, Langur and Asiatic Lion. Although most people can associate with the lion as the king of the savanna in Africa, few are aware of the tiny population of forest lions struggling to survive in the Gir region of Gujarat (my homeland) in Western India.

It is a sobering thought that many people will live their entire lives knowing very little about – or having seen – some of these endangered species in the wild. The human-animal conflict remains the greatest threat to Tulsi the Tiger and his jungle friends.

Loss of habitat, lack of prey, and poaching, are all pushing wildlife to the edge of oblivion. I hope this book will make children and their parents at least think about the plight of these animals; and to find a small space in their hearts for Tulsi Tiger and his friends.

I was fortunate in that my cat, also called Tulsi, has remained loyally by my side every step of the way and has inspired me to set up a small voluntary organisation that provides medical training to frontline rangers working in tiger reserves in India.

The Tulsi Foundation (www.tulsofoundation.co.uk @|TulsiF on Twitter) is named after my beloved cat. It has trained over 1000 rangers, and we hope to increase our support for the men and women who dedicate their lives to the service of Tulsi the Tiger and his jungle friends.

My hope is that the proceeds from this book will help conservation efforts by providing lifesaving medical training for frontline staff.

Chet Trivedy

About the author

Dr Chet Trivedy lives in Kingston-Upon-Thames with his trusted friend Tulsi the cat, and he is not your run-of-the-mill author. He was kidnapped by baboons as a baby and, aged four, he ran away from home to search for cheetahs. Clearly, he was always destined for a career involving wildlife.

At the time of writing (2018) Chet has spent almost 30 years in the healthcare profession as a dentist, a cancer specialist, academic, and consultant in emergency medicine. He is passionate about cricket and works as the crowd doctor for the Kia Oval cricket ground in London.

Somehow, he has also found enough time to turn his hand to conservation. He provides medical support to the Wildlife Conservation Trust (WCT) based in Mumbai, India, and is the founder of the Tulsi Foundation.

The Tulsi Foundation is a voluntary, non-profit organisation set up in 2016 to support the health of frontline staff who work and live in the jungles of India. To date the Tulsi Foundation – with the support of the WCT – has trained over 1,100 rangers in fourteen tiger reserves across three states in Central India.

These rangers play a key role in keeping Tulsi the tiger and his jungle friends safe; and help ensure these precious animals will survive to enthral future generations.

This book was written while the author was recovering from a stroke and sought refuge in the company of the tigers at his local zoo. The stories also showcase some of the lesser known species of Indian wildlife such as the dhole, gaur, Asiatic lion, and the vulture.

As a doctor and conservationist Chet has been able to subtly weave many of his story's themes around health, wellbeing, and conservation, all told through the antics of Tulsi's brave, enigmatic, loveable – and often naughty – friends.

He explains, '*Tulsi the Tiger & Stories of his Jungle Friends* was written to help children gain a better understanding and appreciation of the wonderful wildlife that surrounds us. The term "One Health" is a concept which helps us acknowledge that our own health is deeply intertwined with the health of the animals and the planet we all share.

'All profits from the sale of this book will be invested into the work of the Tulsi Foundation to support those rangers working in tiger reserves, plus grass root projects in and around conservation areas designed to help local children better understand the vital importance of the magical creatures around them.'

More information about the Tulsi Foundation can be found at www.tulsifoundation.co.uk

In the Presence of My Lord

By Chet Trivedy

As the first rays of dawn trickle through the canopy of ghost trees the forest floor is lit with the sparkle of molten emeralds.

The distant call of a sambar heralds the arrival of our Lord, unseen and unheard, but whose unmistaken majestic presence resonates to every being around.

Those blessed by the fleeting vision of black and gold can only marvel at his splendour; but for me, I am content just to bask in the radiance of his invisible form, safe in the knowledge that he is close by.

And that I can follow in his footsteps, breathe the same air, and share the same space; praying that one day I will be blessed once again to bask in the presence of my Lord.

Homage to the Indian jungle – Tadoba, November 2014

First published 2019
Published by GB Publishing.org

Cover Design © 2019
Illustrations by © Derek Pearson, 2019

GBP.

GB Publishing Org
www.gbpublishing.co.uk

CPSIA information can be obtained
at www.ICGtesting.com
Printed in the USA
LVHW101550310519
619762LV00007B/166/P